Alphabet Age 3-5

Carol Medcalf & Becky Hempstock

In a strange place, not too far from here, lives a scare of monsters.

A 'scare' is what some people call a group of monsters, but these monsters are really very friendly once you get to know them.

They are a curious bunch – they look very unusual, but they are quite like you and me, and they love learning new things and having fun.

In this book you will go on a learning journey with the monsters and you are sure to have lots of fun along the way.

Do not forget to visit our website to find out more about all the monsters and to send us photos of you in your monster mask or the monsters that you draw and make!

Contents

Letter a

Mum is helping Nano to learn his letters. **a** is the first letter of the **a**lphabet. Sing the **a**lphabet song with Mum **a**nd Nano.

'**a**bcdefg, hijklmnop, qrs, tuv, wx, y **a**nd z, now I know my **a**bc, come **a**long **a**nd sing with me.'

1 Circle the letter **a** on the **a**lphabet line **a**t the bottom of the page.

2 Start **a**t the red dot **a**nd join the dots below to write **a**.

a a a a a a a

3 Draw lines to match the letter **a** to **a**ll the pictures that begin with **a**.

a

abcdefghijklmnopqrstuvwxyz

Letter b

b is the second letter of
the alphabet.
All these words start with
the letter **b**.
Nano is a **b**aby and he
likes **b**ouncing his **b**lue **b**all,
boing, **b**oing, **b**oing.

1 Circle the letter **b** on the alphabet line at the **b**ottom of the page.

2 Join the dots **b**elow to write **b**.

b b b b b b

3 Colour the pictures that start with the letter **b**.
Colour using **b**lue and **b**rown.
They **b**oth start with **b**.

abcdefghijklmnopqrstuvwxyz

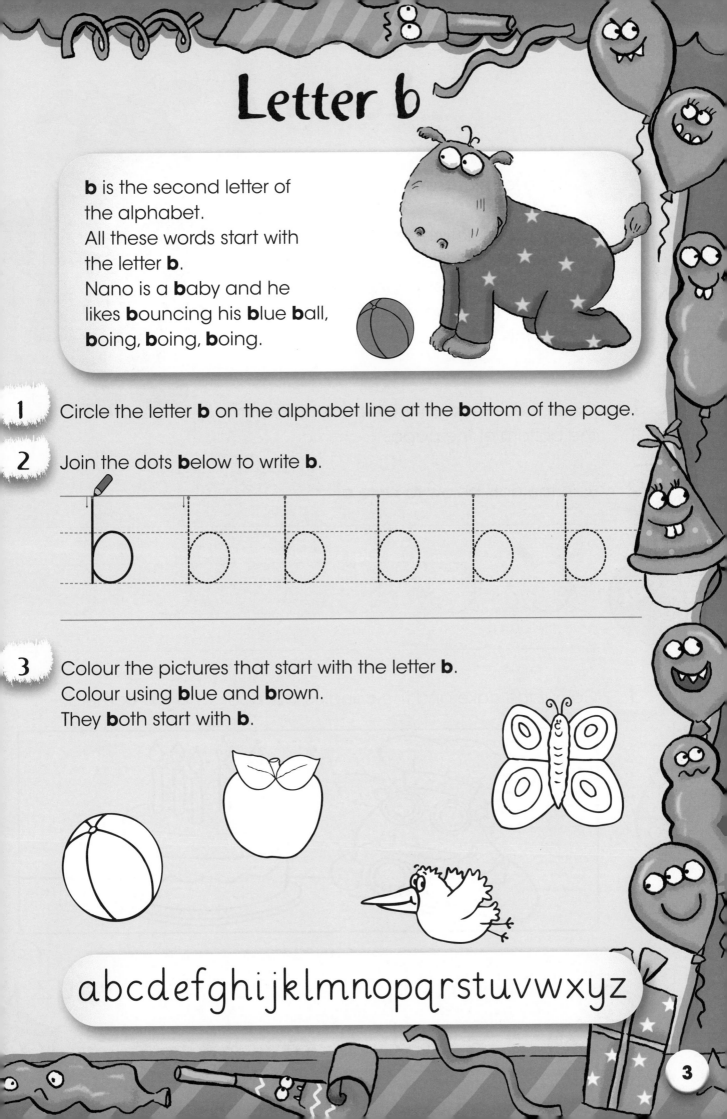

Letter c

Tizz loves her **c**amera and **c**ooking.
She takes pictures of a **c**ake she baked for Nano.
Tizz puts **c**andles on the **c**ake.
Think of more words that start with this letter sound.

1 Circle the letter **c** on the alphabet line at the bottom of the page.

2 Join the dots below to write **c**.

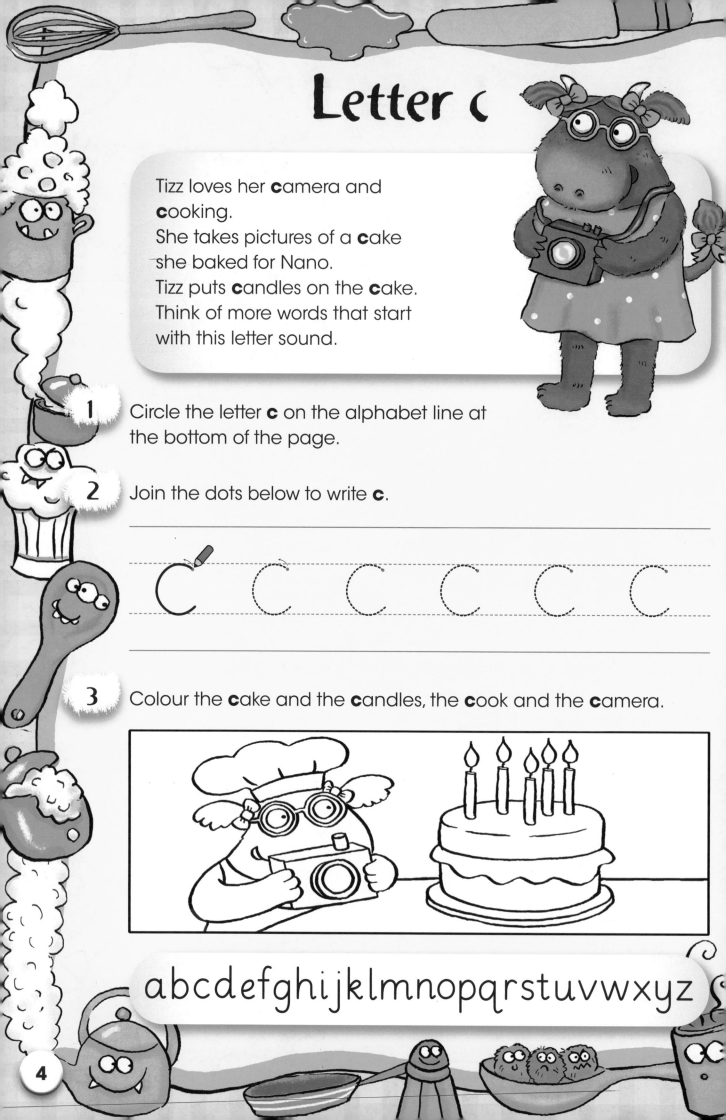

3 Colour the **c**ake and the **c**andles, the **c**ook and the **c**amera.

abcdefghijklmnopqrstuvwxyz

Fun Zone!

Monster alphabet soup

This activity will help your child to learn the sound of the first letter of a word by saying the sound.

What you will need

A bowl, a wooden spoon, toys and objects starting with the same letter, such as **c**ar, **c**at, **c**rown, **c**one, **c**up.

They can also use pictures of objects that begin with the same letter.

What to do

1. Place the objects/pictures in the bowl.
2. Stir the objects/pictures with the wooden spoon.
3. Make up a cooking rhyme with your child, such as:

   'Hubble bubble, I am cooking a monster soup,
   I am putting in a car, **c**, **c**, **c**, stir, stir, stir.
   I am cooking a monster soup,
   I am putting in a cat, **c**, **c**, **c**, stir, stir, stir . . .'

Alternatives

Add in an object/picture that does not begin with the letter **c**, such as a spoon. Explain to your child why that object should not go in – a spoon starts with a '**s**', not a '**c**', sound.

More ideas

Try making soup for all the letters they have learned so far.

Examples include apple, arrow, ball, book, box, butterfly.

> Excellent! Now your child can find and colour **Shape 1** on the Monster Match page!

5

Letter d

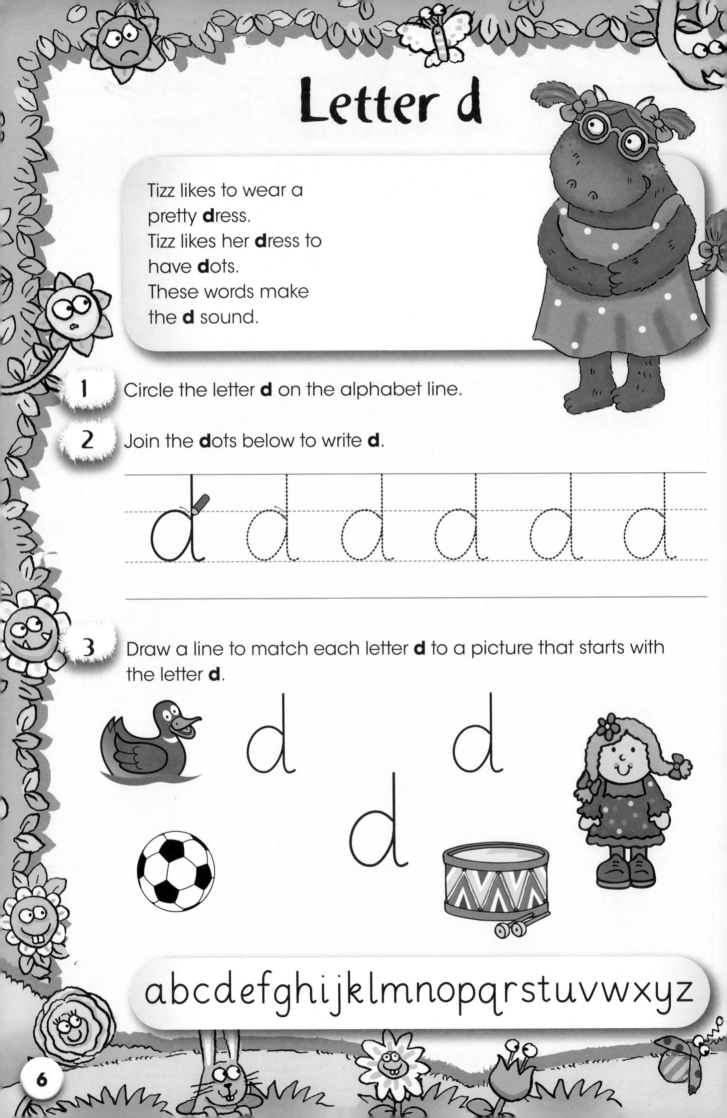

Tizz likes to wear a
pretty **d**ress.
Tizz likes her **d**ress to
have **d**ots.
These words make
the **d** sound.

1 Circle the letter **d** on the alphabet line.

2 Join the **d**ots below to write **d**.

d d d d d d d

3 Draw a line to match each letter **d** to a picture that starts with
the letter **d**.

d   d

d

abcdefghijklmnopqrstuvwxyz

Letter e

Kora **e**njoys
eating **e**ggs.
Do you **e**njoy
eating **e**ggs?
Eggs give you lots of
energy for **e**xercise.

1 Circl**e** th**e** letter **e** on th**e** alphabet lin**e**.

2 Join th**e** dots below to writ**e e**.

e e e e e e

3 Help Kora draw a lin**e** to join up all th**e** pictures
that start with th**e** letter **e**.
Finish at th**e** big **e**.

abcdefghijklmnopqrstuvwxyz

Letter f

When I am not in my science lab
I like to go **f**ishing, or **f**lying in
a plane.
Fishing is **f**un.
Flying is **f**antastic.
Say the **f** sound with me.

1 Circle the letter **f** on the alphabet line.

2 Join the dots below to write **f**.

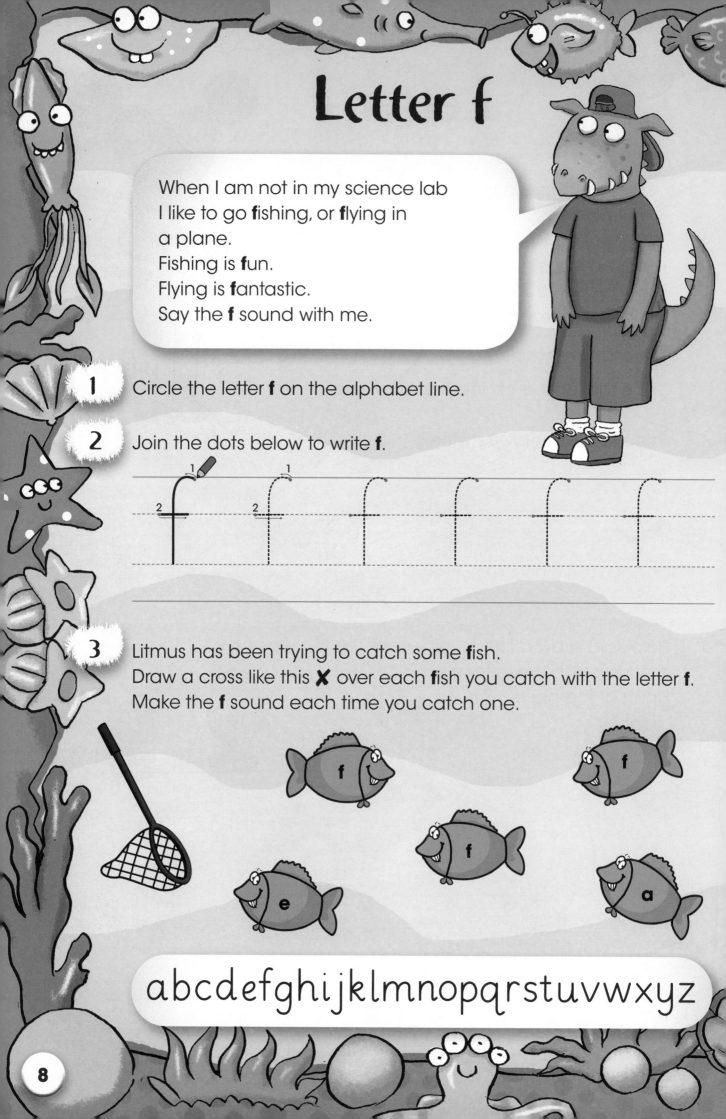

3 Litmus has been trying to catch some **f**ish.
Draw a cross like this ✗ over each **f**ish you catch with the letter **f**.
Make the **f** sound each time you catch one.

abcdefghijklmnopqrstuvwxyz

Fun Zone!

Aeroplane chase

This activity will help your child to say, hear and learn each letter sound as you pass each one in turn.

What to do

1 Chase Webber's aeroplane around the alphabet sky.
2 Help your child to trace with their finger or write with their pencil to catch each letter as they pass.
3 Say the letter names out loud together.
4 Link the letters to the words in the boxes.

| apple | dog | ant | cat | elephant |

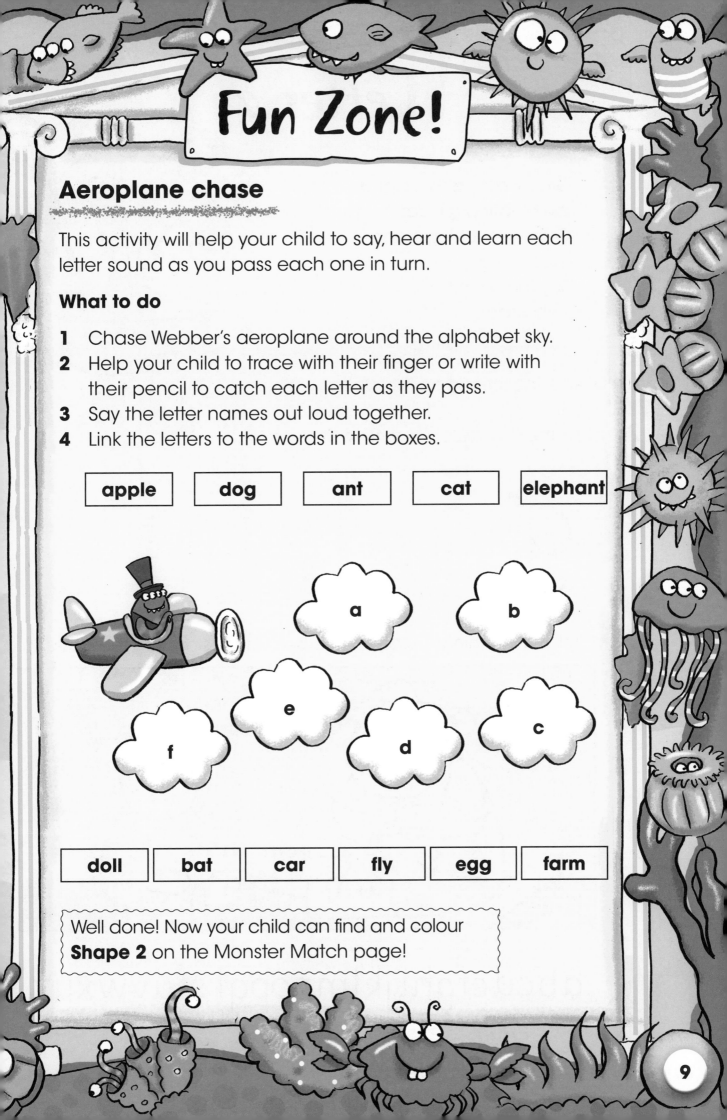

a

b

e

c

f

d

| doll | bat | car | fly | egg | farm |

Well done! Now your child can find and colour
Shape 2 on the Monster Match page!

Letter g

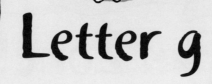

Gran wears **g**lasses and loves eating **g**rapes. Gran is teaching Nano the letter **g**. Say the **g** sound with Gran.

1 Circle the letter **g** on the alphabet line.

2 Join the dots below to write **g**.

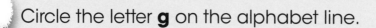

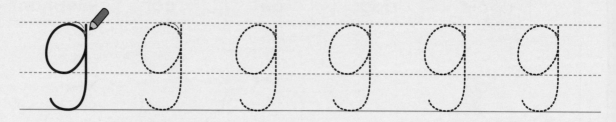

3 Circle all the things in the picture below that start with the **g** sound.

abcdefghijklmnopqrstuvwxyz

Letter h

Grandpa spends a lot of time fixing **h**oles in the **h**ouse. Holes and **h**ouse both make the **h** sound.
Say the **h** sound with Grandpa.

1 Circle the letter **h** on the alphabet line.

2 Join the dots below to write **h**.

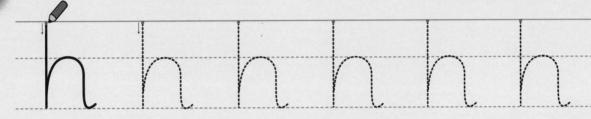

3 Grandpa **h**as lots of **h**ats.
Colour each **h**at and say the **h** sound.

abcdefghijklmnopqrstuvwxyz

Letter i

Fizz is telling Nano about the
letter **i** in her name.
Fizz **i**s careful teaching
the **i** sound.
Sometimes **i**t says **i** as in **i**nk,
sometimes **i** as in **i**ce cream.
In the winter, Fizz builds **i**gloos.

1 Circle the letter **i** on the alphabet line.

2 Join the dots below to write **i**.

3 Follow the trail of **i**ndigo **i**ce cream and join up all the pictures
that start with the letter **i**.

abcdefghijklmnopqrstuvwxyz

Fun Zone!

Monster letters

This activity will help your child to make and recognise letters.

You will need

A pencil, scissors, wool, glue and card or paper.

What to do

1 Draw large lower-case letters on a piece of paper or card with a pencil.
2 Cut the letters out.
3 Let your child put glue all over the letters.
4 Help your child decorate the letters using wool.

Alternatives

You may be able to think of lots more materials you can use to make letters.

Instead of using glue, you could ask your child to paint using different colours within the letter shapes.

More ideas

Help your child to create the letters to spell their own name or make letters to spell someone else's name for a greetings card.

Super! Now your child can find and colour **Shape 3** on the Monster Match page!

Letter j

Leckie loves **j**elly.
She loves to **j**ump, **j**uggle
and **j**og.
The **j** sound is Leckie's
favourite sound.

1 Circle the letter **j** on the alphabet line.

2 Join the dots below to write **j**.

3 Colour everything that starts with the **j** sound.

abcdefghijklmnopqrstuvwxyz

Letter k

Kora's name starts with the letter **k**.
Kora says the letter **k** is sometimes called **k**icking **k** as it looks like it is **k**icking.
It also makes the same sound as the letter c.
Be careful as the two letters are often mixed up.

1 Circle the letter **k** on the alphabet line.

2 Join the dots below to write **k**.

k k k k k k

3 Draw a football for each **k**icking **k**.
Kora has done the first one for you.

k k k

abcdefghijklmnopqrstuvwxyz

Letter l

Nano **l**oves playing
with **L**eckie.
He also **l**ikes to **l**ick **l**ollies
but **L**itmus says he is
too **l**ittle.

1 Circle the letter **l** on the alphabet line.

2 Join the dots below to write **l**.

3 Draw a circle around each object that starts with **l**.
Colour the objects in using **l**ight colours.

abcdefghijklmnopqrstuvwxyz

Fun Zone!

Spot the difference

This activity will help to develop your child's hand-eye coordination and counting skills.

What to do

1   Ask your child to look at these two pictures of Nano.
2   There are five differences between the two pictures.
3   Help your child to circle them all on the second picture.

Monsterific! Now your child can find and colour
Shape 4 on the Monster Match page!

Letter m

Mum wants to teach Nano the letter **m**.
The word '**M**u**m**' starts and ends with the letter **m**.
Say the **m** sound with **M**u**m**.

1 Circle the letter **m** on the alphabet line.

2 Join the dots below to write **m**.

m m m m m

3 Nano is lost in this **m**onster **m**aze and wants to get home.
Follow the path through the **m**aze past all the pictures that start with the letter **m**.

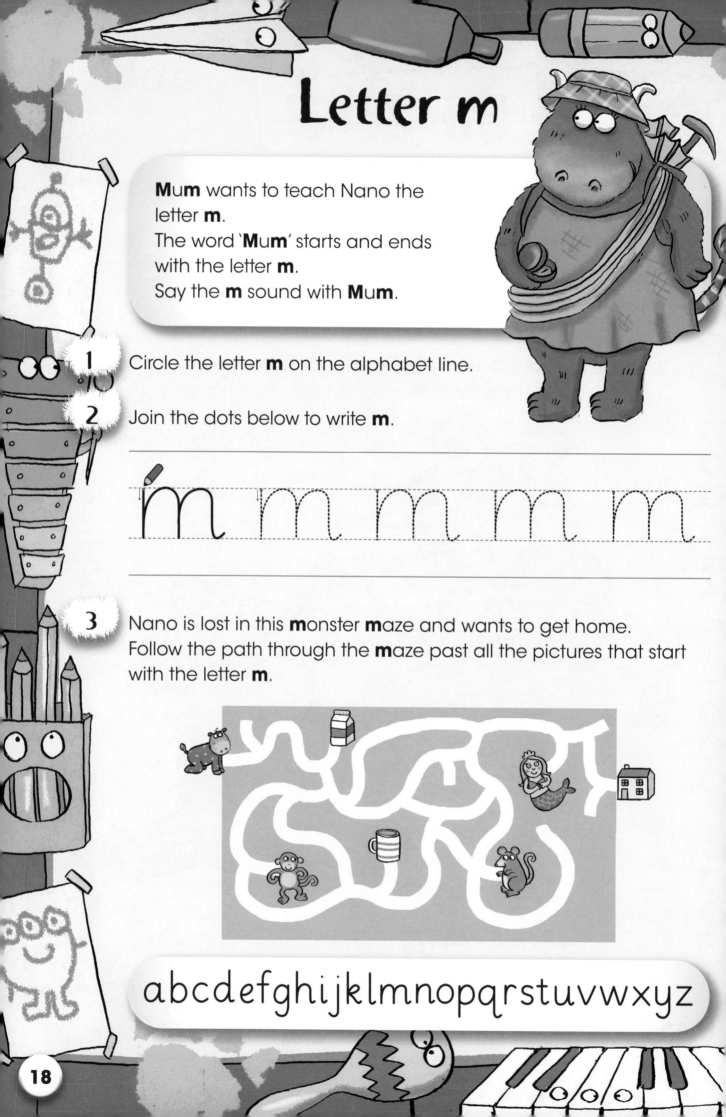

abcdefghijklmnopqrstuvwxyz

Letter n

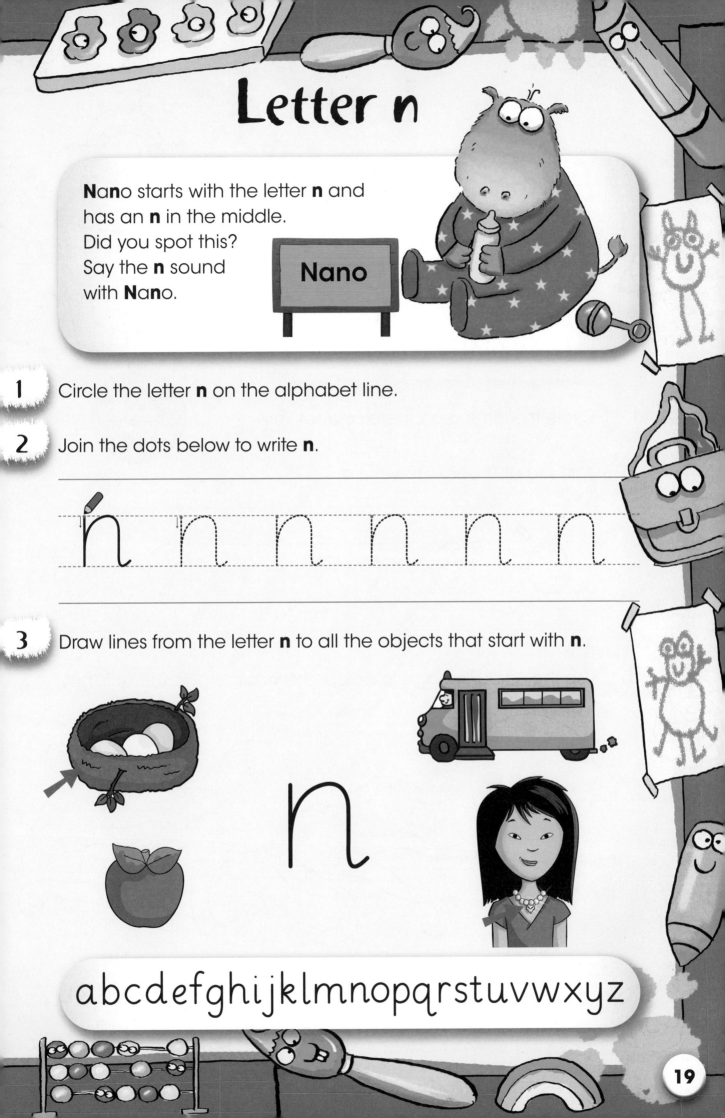

Nano starts with the letter **n** and has an **n** in the middle.
Did you spot this?
Say the **n** sound with **N**a**n**o.

Nano

1 Circle the letter **n** on the alphabet line.

2 Join the dots below to write **n**.

n n n n n n

3 Draw lines from the letter **n** to all the objects that start with **n**.

n

abcdefghijklmnopqrstuvwxyz

19

Letter o

I am **Otto** and I love the letter **o**.
I like circles t**oo** because my wheel is a circle and it helps me move around.
Make your arms g**o** round in big circles in the air.

1 Circle the letter **o** on the alphabet line.

2 Join the dots below to write **o**.

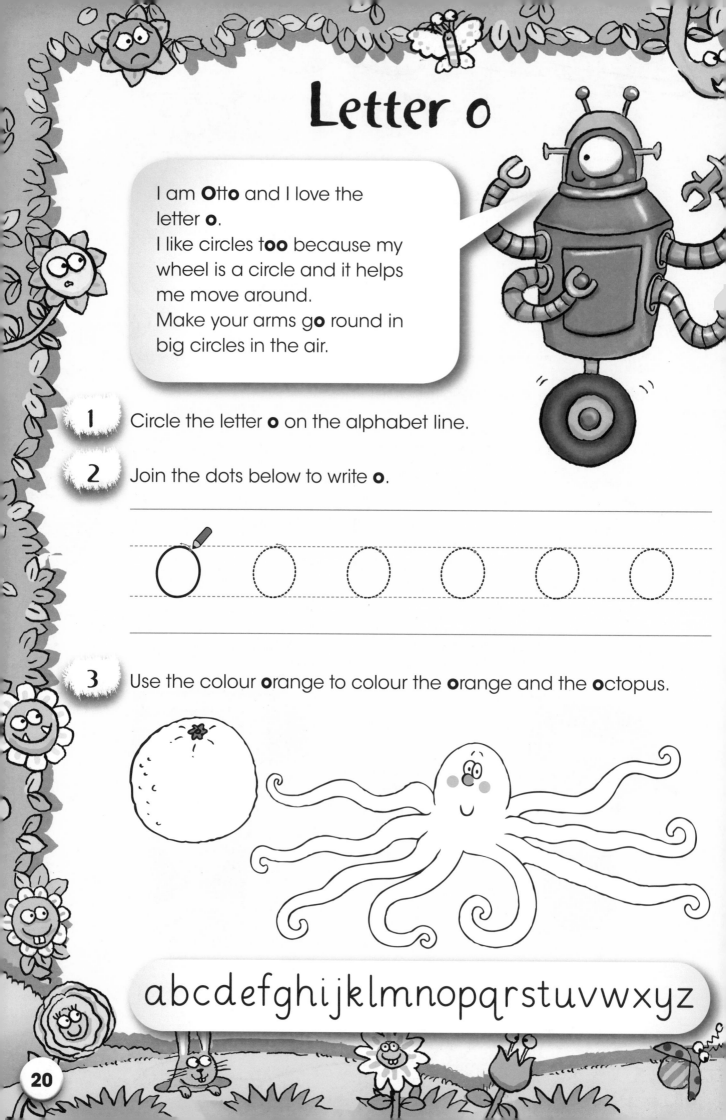

3 Use the colour **o**range to colour the **o**range and the **o**ctopus.

abcdefghijklmnopqrstuvwxyz

Fun Zone!

Alphabet book

This activity will help your child to match all the letters of the alphabet to pictures that start with each letter.

You will need

A4 plain paper, a black crayon, scissors, glue and lots of old magazines, pictures or greetings cards.

What to do

1 Fold the A4 paper in half to make a book.
2 Add enough sheets so that each letter of the alphabet has a page of its own.
3 Ask your child to design a front cover. You could suggest calling it 'Nano's Alphabet Book'.
4 Write a letter at the top of each page.
5 Ask your child to find as many pictures as they can that start with that letter.
6 Cut out the pictures for them and help them to stick the pictures on to the pages.

Alternatives

Your child could use real objects to represent letters, e.g. a leaf or an old lolly stick for l.

More ideas

If your child cannot find anything to illustrate a particular letter, they can draw their own picture.

Brilliant! Now your child can find and colour **Shape 5** on the Monster Match page!

Letters p and q

Dad and Nano are in the **p**ark.
They see some ducks in the **p**ond.
They are **q**uacking very loudly!

Dad says the letter **q** is usually followed by the letter u.
Together they make the **q**u sound.

1 Circle the letters **p** and **q** on the alphabet line.

2 Join the dots below to write **p**.

p p p p p p

3 Join the dots below to write **q**.

q q q q q q

abcdefghijklmnopqrstuvwxyz

Letter r

Otto is a **r**obot monster.
He **r**olls around Monsterville helping Grandpa to fix things.
His a**r**ms are bendy and he can make the shape of an **r**.
He is teaching Nano the **r** sound and **r**oa**r**s like a lion!
Say **r, r, r, r**oa**r**.

1 Circle the lette**r r** on the alphabet line.

2 Join the dots below to write **r**.

r r r r r r

3 Draw circles around the objects that start with the **r** sound.

abcdefghijklmnopqrstuvwxyz

Letter s

Poggo love**s** his **s**ister**s**,
skateboard and pet **s**nake.
Poggo's **s**nake often make**s**
the **s s**hape.
Poggo **s**ays 'Hi**ss** like a **s**nake'.

1 Circle the letter **s** on the alphabet line.

2 Join the dot**s** below to write **s**.

s s s s s s

3 Draw a line to link all the object**s** that **s**tart with the **s s**ound.

start

stop

abcdefghijklmnopqrstuvwxyz

Fun Zone!

Silly, slinky snakes

This activity will help your child to order all the letters of the alphabet.

You will need

Old egg boxes, string, paint, pens and crayons.

What to do

1 Cut out the parts of the egg boxes that the eggs sit in.
2 Help your child to decorate the egg cups with paint and leave to dry.
3 Make a hole in the top of each egg cup.
4 Help your child thread the string through all the parts together to make the snake – it can be as long as you like.
5 Secure the last egg cup with a knot.
6 Help your child to write one letter on each egg cup.
   Write the letters in alphabetical order.

Alternatives

Instead of using old egg boxes, you could make a paper chain snake using loops of paper joined together.

More ideas

Write letters on each section of the snake to make words.

Splendid! Now your child can find and colour **Shape 6** on the Monster Match page!

Letter t

Tizz loves **t**aking photos.
She also likes playing **t**ennis
with her sister Fizz.
t is the nex**t** letter in **t**he
alphabe**t**.
Say the **t** sound with Tizz.

1 Circle the letter **t** on **t**he alphabe**t** line.

2 Join **t**he dots below **t**o write **t**.

t t t t t t

3 Find and circle all the **t**hings in the picture **t**hat start with **t**he **t** sound.

abcdefghijklmnopqrstuvwxyz

26

Letters u, v and w

Webber always **u**ses his **u**mbrella **w**hen it rains.
His **u**mbrella is **v**ery **u**seful as he never gets **w**et.

1 Circle the letters **u**, **v** and **w** on the alphabet line.

2 Join the dots below to write **u** and colour the picture.

3 Join the dots below to write **v** and colour the picture.

4 Join the dots below to **w**rite **w** and colour the picture.

abcdefghijklmnopqrstuvwxyz

Letters x, y and z

Nano is playing hide and seek
with Zak in the kitchen.
Zak hides in a bo**x**!
After the game, Nano is tired.
He **y**awns and falls asleep, **z**, **z**, **z**.

1   Circle the letters **x**, **y** and **z** on the alphabet line.

2   Join the dots below to write letter **x**.

X x x x x

3   Join the dots below to write letter **y**.

y y y y y

4   Join the dots below to write letter **z**.

z z z z z

abcdefghijklmnopqrstuvwxyz

Fun Zone!

Alphabet search

This activity will help your child to find and recognise letters and to say their sounds.

What to do

1 All the letters of the alphabet are hidden in this picture.

2 Help your child to find and circle them all. There are 26 to find.

3 Help them cross each letter off the alphabet line on page 28 as they find them.

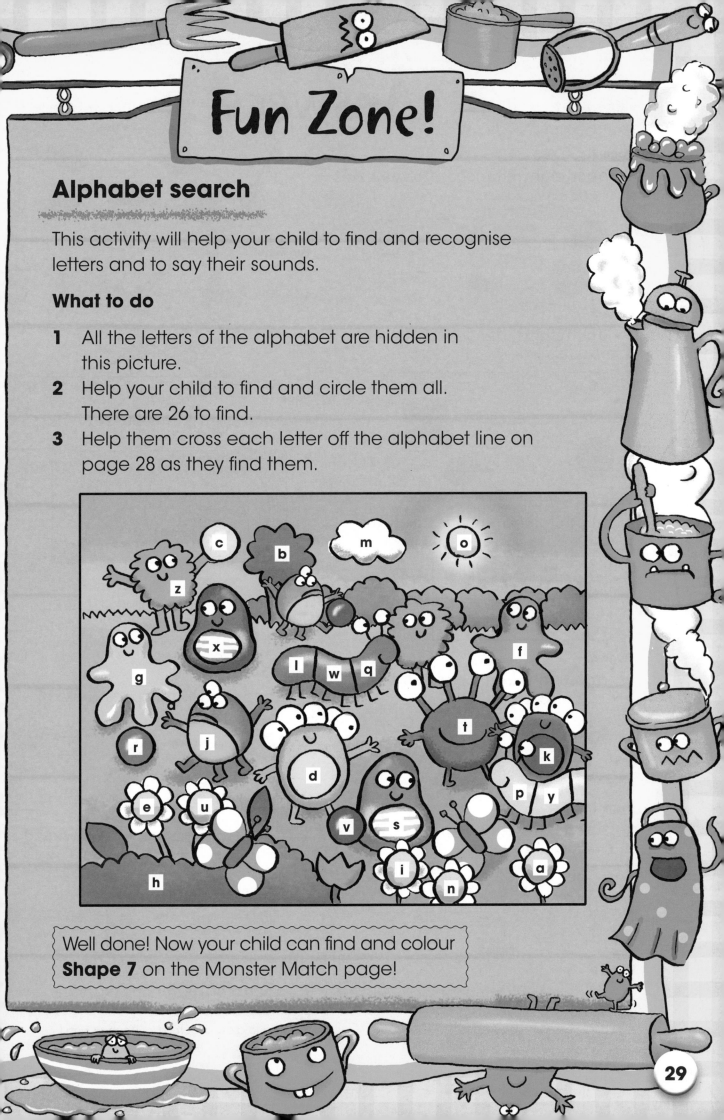

Well done! Now your child can find and colour **Shape 7** on the Monster Match page!

Answers

Page 2

1 @bcdefghijklmnopqrstuvwxyz

2 Child to join the dots

3

Page 3

1 a(b)cdefghijklmnopqrstuvwxyz

2 Child to join the dots

3 The following objects to be coloured either blue, brown or both

Page 4

1 ab(c)defghijklmnopqrstuvwxyz

2 Child to join the dots

3

Page 6

1 abc(d)efghijklmnopqrstuvwxyz

2 Child to join the dots

3

Page 7

1 abcd(e)fghijklmnopqrstuvwxyz

2 Child to join the dots

3

Page 8

1 abcde(f)ghijklmnopqrstuvwxyz

2 Child to join the dots

3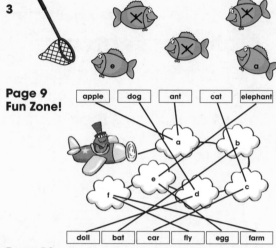

Page 9
Fun Zone!

Page 10

1 abcdef(g)hijklmnopqrstuvwxyz

2 Child to join the dots

3

Page 11

1 abcdefg(h)ijklmnopqrstuvwxyz

2 Child to join the dots

3 Child to colour each of the hats and say the h sound

Page 12

1 abcdefgh(i)jklmnopqrstuvwxyz

2 Child to join the dots

3

Page 14

1 abcdefghi(j)klmnopqrstuvwxyz

2 Child to join the dots

3

Page 15

1 abcdefghij(k)lmnopqrstuvwxyz

2 Child to join the dots

3 Child to draw a football for each kicking k

Page 16

1 abcdefghij**k**lmnopqrstuvwxyz

2 Child to join the dots

3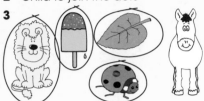

Page 17

Fun Zone

Page 18

1 abcdefghijkl**m**nopqrstuvwxyz

2 Child to join the dots

3

Page 19

1 abcdefghijklm**n**opqrstuvwxyz

2 Child to join the dots

3

Page 20

1 abcdefghijklmn**o**pqrstuvwxyz

2 Child to join the dots

3

Page 22

1 abcdefghijklmno**p**qrstuvwxyz

2 Child to join the dots

3 Child to join the dots

Page 23

1 abcdefghijklmnop**qr**stuvwxyz

2 Child to join the dots

3

Page 24

1 abcdefghijklmnopqr**s**tuvwxyz

2 Child to join the dots

3

Page 26

1 abcdefghijklmnopqrs**t**uvwxyz

2 Child to join the dots

3

Page 27

1 abcdefghijklmnopqrstu**vw**xyz

2 Child to join the dots and colour the picture

3 Child to join the dots and colour the picture

4 Child to join the dots and colour the picture

Page 28

1 abcdefghijklmnopqrstuvw**xyz**

2 Child to join the dots

3 Child to join the dots

4 Child to join the dots

Page 29
Fun Zone!

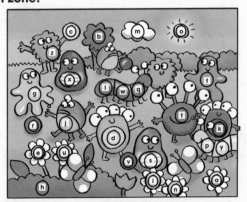

Monster Match

Each time your child completes a topic in this book, they will be awarded a shape number.

Help your child to find and colour the shapes in the picture of Leckie that match the numbers they have been given.

As your child works through the book they will gradually see Leckie come to life!